D1238912

Walter Warthog's Wonderful Wagon

by Barbara deRubertis • illustrated by R.W. Alley

THE KANE PRESS / NEW YORK

Alpha Betty's Class

Alexander Anteater

Bobby Baboon

Corky Cub

Dilly Dog

Hanna Hippo

Eddie Elephant

Frances Frog

Gertie Gorilla

Lana Llama

Izzy Impala

Jeremy Jackrabbit

Kylie Kangaroo

Maxwell Moose

Library of Congress Cataloging-in-Publication Data

deRubertis, Barbara.
Walter Warthog's wonderful wagon / by Barbara deRubertis ; illustrated by R.W. Alley.
p. cm. — (Animal antics A to Z)
Summary: Walter Warthog works hard to earn money so he can buy the wonderful white wagon in
the hardware store.
ISBN 978-1-57565-356-3 (library binding : alk. paper) — ISBN 978-1-57565-348-8 (pbk. : alk. paper) —
ISBN 978-1-57565-387-7 (e-book)
[1. Moneymaking projects—Fiction. 2. Wagons—Fiction. 3. Warthog—Fiction. 4. Animals—Fiction.
5. Alphabet.] I. Alley, R. W. (Robert W.), ill. II. Title.
PZ7.D4475Wal 2011
[E]—dc22   2010051322

1 3 5 7 9 10 8 6 4 2

First published in the United States of America in 2011 by Kane Press, Inc.
Printed in the United States of America
WOZ0711

Series Editor: Juliana Hanford
Book Design: Edward Miller

Animal Antics A to Z is a registered trademark of Kane Press, Inc.

www.kanepress.com

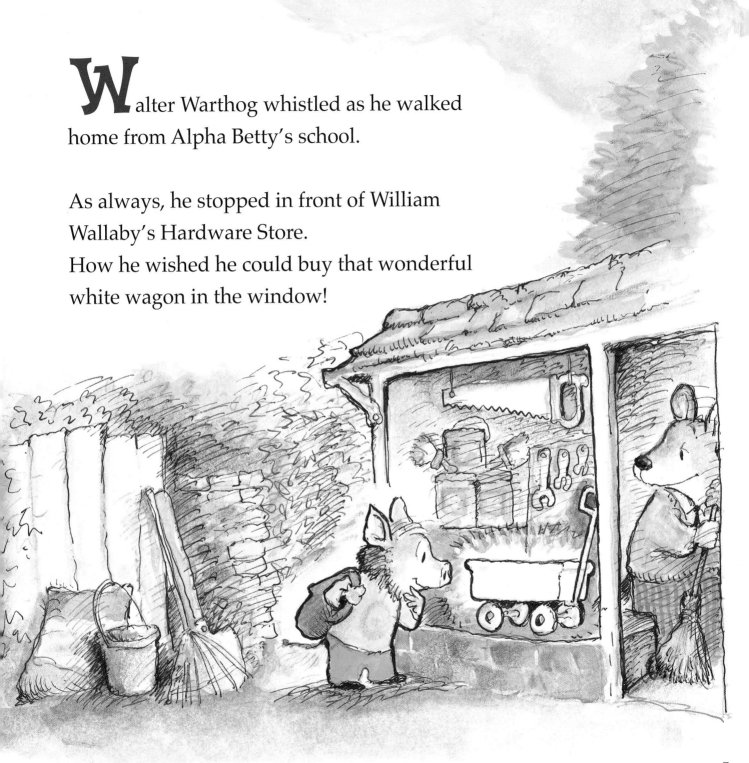

Walter Warthog whistled as he walked home from Alpha Betty's school.

As always, he stopped in front of William Wallaby's Hardware Store.
How he wished he could buy that wonderful white wagon in the window!

William Wallaby saw Walter and waved him inside.

"You really want that white wagon, don't you, Walter," said William.

"Oh, yes! I do!" Walter whispered.
"But I don't have any money."

William said, "Well, I have an idea.
Why don't you ask your parents if you can
make deliveries for me after school?
You could *earn* the money to buy the wagon."

Walter whooped wildly. "OKAY!"

Walter's parents liked the idea. So Walter hurried
to the hardware store the next day after school.
But the wagon was not in the window!

"Oh, NO!" Walter wailed. "Someone bought
my wagon!"

Walter rushed inside. And there was William . . .
loading up the wagon!

"Please deliver these watering cans to Wendy
Wombat's Watermelon Patch," William said.
Then he winked. "You can *use* the wagon to
earn the money to *buy* the wagon!"

Walter happily wound his way down the road.
The wagon wheels whirred behind him like music.

Walter quickly arrived at the watermelon patch.
"Here are your watering cans!" he called to
Wendy Wombat.

"What a wonderful wagon!" said Wendy.

"It's not mine yet," Walter said. "I'm working
for the money to buy it."

"You can earn some money from me," said Wendy.
"Just take these four watermelons to Wanda
Weasel's Water Park."

Walter beamed. "Thanks, Wendy!"

Four watermelons weighed a lot!

The wagon went whizzing DOWN the hill.

But pulling the wagon UP the hill was hard work!

Walter was wet with sweat when he arrived at
Wanda Weasel's Water Park.

He found Wanda painting flower boxes.
"Wow!" said Wanda. "What a wonderful wagon!"

"I'm working for William Wallaby to buy it,"
said Walter.

"Well, you look worn out," Wanda said.
"Why don't you whip down the water slide!"

Walter quickly washed off in the shower.
Then he **WHOOSHED** down the water slide.
And he landed with a whopping **WHUP** in the
swimming pool.

"Now you can earn some money from me!"
said Wanda. "Please take these old water skis
back to William's hardware store.
Ask him to order another pair just like them."

"Thanks, Wanda!" said Walter. He felt very happy.
Soon this wonderful wagon would be his!

Walter whistled as he went back to
William's store.

Suddenly little Warren Wolverine swerved
around the corner on his bike.
He **WHUMPED** into the wagon!

Warren fell off his bike and began wailing!

Walter sat down beside Warren on the sidewalk.
"I can take you home in the wagon," Walter said.
"The front wheel of your bike looks wobbly."

"Thanks, Walter," Warren whimpered.
"I'm sorry I walloped your wagon.
It looks even worse than my bike!"

Walter wiped his hand over the chipped white paint.
His eyes watered up. What should he do?

Walter loaded Warren and the bike into the wagon.
And he worried all the way to Warren's house.

But Warren was having a wonderful time!
"Wheeee!" he sang out. "Go FASTER, Walter!"

23

Finally Walter returned to the hardware store.
He told William Wallaby what had happened.

"I've been thinking about ways to fix the wagon,"
Walter said. "I promise I'll take care of it."

Then Walter added, "I earned some extra money today." He held it out to William.

William smiled. "You're a good worker, Walter. And you're very responsible. I'm proud of you."

A few days later, Walter delivered the new
water skis to Wanda Weasel.
She was painting the fence when he arrived.

"Whoa!" said Wanda. "What happened to
your wagon?"

Walter explained.

Then he said, "Wanda, I've been wondering.
Would you be willing to do a 'work swap'?
I'll make deliveries for you . . . if you'll help me
paint the wagon."

"Wonderful idea!" said Wanda. "Let's go to work!"

Soon the white wagon looked as good as new.

And in a few weeks, Walter had done enough
work to pay for it!

The wagon reads: "Walter Warthog's Wagon Deliveries"

By then Walter had many customers. So he started his
OWN business: *Walter Warthog's Wagon Deliveries*!

Walter continued working for William.
And Wanda. And Wendy. And many others.
Even Walter's teacher, Alpha Betty, would hire
him from time to time!

Walter's wagon was useful in so many ways!

But most of all, he loved giving his friends rides
in his wonderful white wagon.

And they loved giving Walter Warthog rides, too!

Walter Warthog's
Wagon Deliveries

STAR OF THE BOOK: THE WARTHOG

FUN FACTS

- Home: Warthogs are wild pigs that live in African grasslands.
- Size: Warthogs range from three to four feet in length and from 100 to 300 pounds in weight.
- Appearance: The warthog's "warts" are really two pairs of wart-like bumps on the sides of their heads. Warthogs also have two pairs of long, curving tusks. The tusks on the upper jaw can grow to be more than two feet long!
- **Did You Know?** Warthogs are powerful diggers! They are also fast runners and excellent jumpers!

LOOK BACK

Learning to identify letter sounds (phonemes) at the beginning, middle, and end of words is called "phonemic awareness."

- The word *wish* has the *w* sound at the <u>beginning</u> of the word. Listen to the words on page 5 being read again. When you hear a word that <u>begins</u> with the *w* sound, wiggle your fingers over your head and say the word.
- The word *shower* has the *w* sound in the <u>middle</u> of the word. Listen to the first sentence on page 16 being read again. When you hear a word that has the *w* sound in the <u>middle</u>, wiggle your fingers in front of your tummy and say the word.

TRY THIS!

Make Wagon Words!

- On 9 separate sheets of paper, print a large green *w*, the **red vowels** *e* and *i*, and the **black consonants** *b, d, g, ll, n*, and *t*.
- Set three chairs side by side to make a wagon. The person in the first chair holds the *w*. The person in the middle chair holds the *e* and *i*. And the person in the last chair holds the *b, d, g, ll, n*, and *t*.
- The first person holds up *w*. The second person holds up *e*. And the third person holds up *b*. Everyone sounds out the word: *w-e-b*. Is it a real word? Thumbs up for "yes," thumbs down for "no." Now the third person holds up each of the other **black consonants** in turn. (Repeat the directions.)
- The second person changes the *e* to *i*. The third person holds up each **black consonant** in turn. (Repeat the directions.)

JUST FOR FUN: When you sound out a word, move the last chair to the first position. Everyone now scoots over one chair. Your "wagon" will move across the room!

FOR MORE ACTIVITIES, go to Walter Warthog's website: www.kanepress.com/AnimalAntics/WalterWarthog.html
You'll also find a recipe for Walter Warthog's Watermelon Punch!